DISNEP
M@ANA 2

Adapted by
Paula Fuga

Illustrated by
Alex Cho

Designed by
Tony Fejeran

A GOLDEN BOOK · NEW YORK

rhcbooks.com

ISBN 978-0-7364-4491-0 (trade) — ISBN 978-0-7364-4492-7 (ebook)

Printed in the United States of America

10 9 8 7 6 5 4 3 2 1

Moana of Motunui raced back to her island in her canoe. She was a master **wayfinder** who loved to explore the ocean.

Motunui was **flourishing**,
and so was Moana's family.
Moana's little sister, Simea,
welcomed her home!

Moana told Simea that their people were great
voyagers. Moana had received a vision that she
must find the lost island, **Motufetū**, and break
an old curse, to connect them all once more.

Simea gave Moana a **sea star** so she could take
a piece of home with her.

An unlikely crew was chosen for Moana's journey:

Moni, a historian who loved tales of Moana's and Maui's adventures,

Kele, a grumpy farmer who would surely keep them fed,

and **Loto**, a canoe-building genius who would keep their vessel in good repair.

Cluck! Cluck!

The entire village gathered along the
shore to bid the new crew **farewell**.

After days on the open sea, Moana recognized danger
in the distance. It was the **Kakamora barge**—home
to dart-blowing, coconut-clad bandits! And behind them
was **a giant clam**!

The canoe was **swallowed** by the clam. The crew went **spiraling downward** in different directions.

The crew slid into a chamber in the clam's belly, landing safely on a **pile of trash**. Moana was separated from them. Where did she go?

Instead of Moana, the crew found the demigod
Maui, who had helped Moana on a quest years
earlier. Moni tried to contain his excitement!

Chee Hoo! Maui was ready to leave the clam.
But then he noticed Heihei and realized that Moana
was in danger. . . .

Meanwhile, Moana was confronted by a demigod named **Matangi**.

She told Moana that they all were *trapped*.

Matangi gave Moana some advice that sounded
like a trick. She said that Moana needed to **get lost**
in order to **find** her way out.

Moana **spun her oar** to clear the darkness
and found a portal.

Maui and the crew burst in. Just then, the
portal opened and sucked everyone into it!

Finally free from the clam, the crew was now in the **cursed sea**.

The ocean around them looked unfamiliar and **sick**. Moana reached into the water and it did not respond.

Motufetū was at the **bottom of the ocean**. How could they reach it? Everyone felt defeated.

Maui dug deep within his heart to cheer Moana up. His encouraging words **lifted her spirits** and the two devised a plan.

To get to Motufetū, the crew had to distract
the god of storms, who was guarding it.

Maui fearlessly used his
magical hook to block
the storm's lightning bolts.

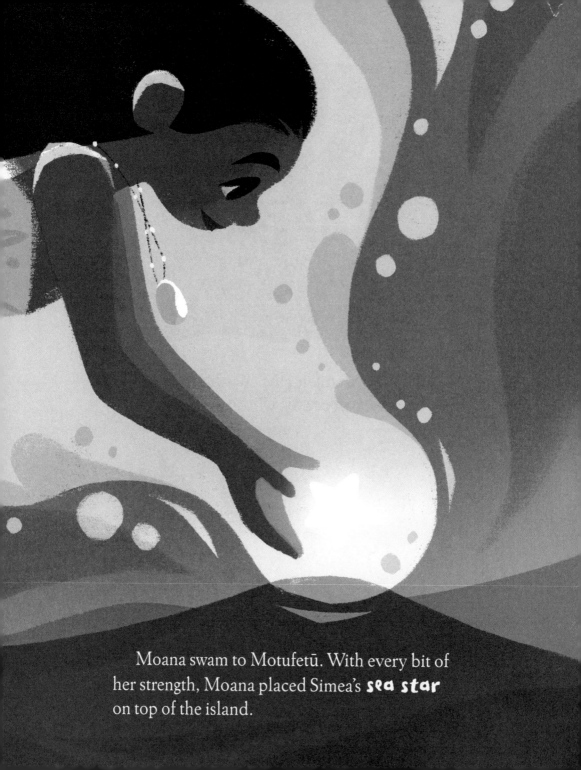

Moana swam to Motufetū. With every bit of
her strength, Moana placed Simea's **sea star**
on top of the island.

Her Gramma Tala's spirit appeared. She was
proud of Moana's bravery.

Maui and Moana pulled Motufetū up from
the ocean, breaking the curse and connecting the
people of the ocean with each other again.

Moana blew her conch shell in **celebration**! **Wayfinders** from every corner of the ocean arrived on the shores of Motufetū.

Moana was happy she could bring all the people of the ocean together and be **reunited with her sister**, Simea!

Moana learned that she could overcome any challenge. She was ready for her next adventure, **wherever the ocean led her**.